Diary of an

ACCIDENTAL

WITCH

NEW GIRL

TO LITTLE WITCHES EVERYWHERE, THIS ONE
IS FOR YOU, H AND P XX

FOR ARCHIE AND OLIVE, MY LOCKDOWN
HEROES, LOVE MUM X

tiger tales

5 River Road, Suite 128, Wilton, CT 06897
Published in the United States 2023
Originally published in Great Britain 2021
by Little Tiger Press Ltd.
Text copyright © 2021 Perdita & Honor Cargill
Illustrations copyright © 2021 Katie Saunders
ISBN-13: 978-1-6643-4057-2
ISBN-10: 1-6643-4057-2
Printed in China
STP/3800/0507/0123
2 4 6 8 10 9 7 5 3 1

www.tigertalesbooks.com

Diary of an ACCIDENTAL WITCH

NEW GIRL

BY PERDITA & HONOR CARGILL

ILLUSTRATED BY KATIE SAUNDERS

tiger tales

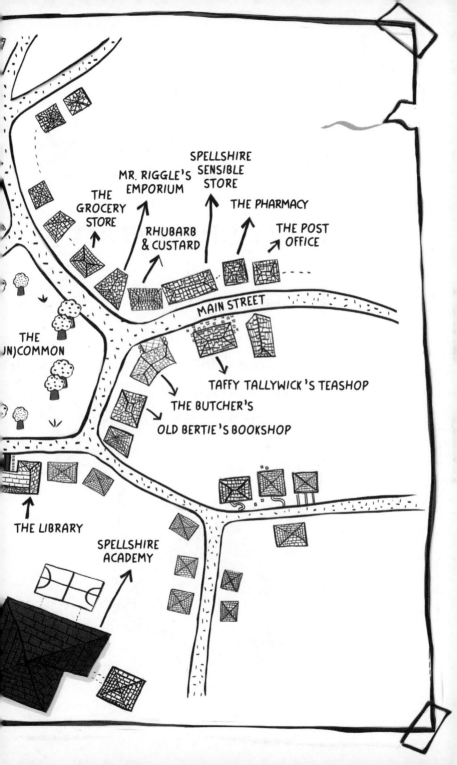

PRIVATE
TOP SECRET

PROPERTY OF BEA BLACK

1 Piggoty Lane,
Little Spellshire,
Spellshire,
Back of Beyond,
Far, far from civilization....

MONDAY SEPTEMBER 13

5:20 p.m. Home

It's our first full day in Little Spellshire, and Dad has given me this diary to "celebrate moving." I know a bribe when I see one—he might be "celebrating," but I never wanted to move here. It's very disappointing how little my opinions count in this family. Who decides to move somewhere just because it has *funny clouds*? Only my dad, that's who.

On the upside, a bribe's a bribe, and I've wanted my own diary since I was in second grade and Milly Strudel had one that smelled like strawberries. This one doesn't smell like anything except new paper, but it's still really nice. I'm going to write down everything that happens to me, and I'm never going to miss a day.

5:43 p.m.

Except ... probably NOTHING will happen to me because now I'm literally living in the middle of nowhere and there's NO RELIABLE PHONE SIGNAL and I don't have any friends. I suppose that means I'll have time to faithfully record all my ~~deep~~ thoughts.

Things I Will ACHIEVE This Year Now That I Have No Friends

- Become a world-famous diarist (must look up other world-famous diarists so I can copy how they do it).
- ~~Learn to speak fluent Italian, Mandarin, and possibly Japanese.~~ (Too tricky.)
- Master all the trickiest soccer skills, especially the Seal Dribble and the Hocus-Pocus.
- ~~Learn to play the piano.~~ (WAY too tricky!)
- Persuade Dad to let me have a puppy.

6:11 p.m.

I HAVE A FRIEND! Well, hopefully....

2

His name is Ashkan (but he says everyone calls him Ash except his mom). He lives next door, and even though his mom had obviously dragged him over to be neighborly, he seems really nice. It was very sunny, so we sat in the yard and had lemonade. Mrs. Namdar wanted to know why we'd moved here, and Dad explained that he was a weather scientist and was writing a book about Little Spellshire's famously freaky microclimate. Then they moved on to schools—Ash is in sixth grade, too—and they talked FOREVER over our heads about how good **Spellshire Academy** is and how it's much better than the other school in town *blah blah blah.*

When they finally took a breath, Ash said he'd show me around the **Academy** after school tomorrow if I wanted (yes!) and asked if I like cupcakes (YES!). Then he went to his house and came back with a plate piled with little green cupcakes he and his mom had baked as a Welcome-to-Piggoty-Lane treat for us.

Then there was a sudden and surprising SNOWSTORM and we all had to run for cover.

6:30 p.m.

It stopped snowing, the sun is scorching again, and we're having the cupcakes for a snack. **Yummy.**

TUESDAY SEPTEMBER 14

2:24 p.m. Home

I only have a few days of **F R E E D O M** before it's back to English and history and math, *ugh!* I'm not meeting Ash for a while, so I'm going to explore Little Spellshire. From what I saw when we drove through town the other day, it's nothing like where we used to live. I asked Dad if I could go on my own and he said of course I could because, if *I* was ever going to turn out to be a scientist, the more exploring I did, the better. I was pretty sure I'd need to be better at actual science to be a scientist, but I didn't argue with him. NO IDEA what I want to "turn out to be," but exploring is one of my MOST favorite things to do.

3:44 p.m. Taffy Tallywick's Teashop

On the upside, I'm sitting writing this in a cozy teashop next to a fire with a little black kitten curled up on my lap. On the downside, unless this storm passes soon, I'm going to be seriously late meeting Ash.

I think it might have been a teeny bit of an understatement when I said Little Spellshire was nothing like where I used to live—it is very, EXCEEDINGLY, UNRECOGNIZABLY different.

For starters, it's **TINY**! Our house is at one end of Piggoty Lane and backs on to the path to the forest (that's my next place to explore), but at the other end—past a bunch of ordinary little houses like ours—the lane comes out on to a funny-shaped green all dotted with trees and pretty weeds named the

Common—or maybe the *Un*Common depending on which sign you believe. There are hardly any people around and only a few cars (mostly orange and bubble-shaped for some strange reason), but there are gazillions of CATS—they're everywhere, curled around street lamps, chilling on mailboxes, and sleeping on the steps of the library.

All around are thatched cottages and wiggly old shops. The shops are NOT what I was hoping for. Most of them are ordinary, if a bit old-fashioned—like the grocery store with its barrels of turnips and red apples outside and a butcher shop with gross dead things hanging in the window. But a few are more ... *peculiar*, like MR. RIGGLE's EMPORIUM, which has a sign in its cloudy glass window saying *GET YOUR FRESH CUCKOO SPIT HERE!* I didn't go into Old Bertie's Bookshop because the old man peering at me from his perch on top of a teetering tower of cobwebby leather books scared me off, and I obviously didn't go into the pub, either (it's named The Moon & Broomstick and it's so covered in ivy that it looks like it's growing out of the ground).

Except for New Street, which is as straight as a ruler and lined mostly with modern houses, all the roads running off the UnCommon are twisty with more wonky old buildings. The Academy is at the end of New Street, so I saved that one for later and checked out Main Street. **Spellshire's Sensible Store** sells boring stuff like beans and bacon and garbage bags, and there's a pharmacy with a sign saying REGULAR PRESCRIPTIONS ONLY and a neat display of nit treatments. But my favorite was Rhubarb & Custard because, as well as selling newspapers, it has CANDY—a whole wall of them in big, old-fashioned, labeled jars.

Toffees

Chocolate eyeballs

Fizzy skullsquigglers*

Fluffmallows**

Through the window of one store, I could see a couple of owls sitting on a branch suspended from the ceiling and a handful of frogs hopping over the counter. But just as I was rattling the handle to see if it was open, the sky went black, there was a peal of thunder so loud several startled cats fell out of trees, and it started to POUR with rain.

*Like jelly beans but much FIZZIER.
**Like marshmallows but much FLUFFIER.

"Quick! In here!" The door of the only tearoom on the street flew open, and an arm reached out and pulled me inside. "You'll get soaked!"

Too late—I was already DRENCHED—but the arm belonged to Taffy, and her tearoom turned out to be a very nice place to shelter. Especially when she brought me a hot chocolate and a big slice of chocolate chip shortbread *for free*. She was very smiley and didn't do that *tut* thing because I wasn't grown up *and* she let me hang my coat and socks by the fireplace to dry out.

I've eaten all the shortbread, the kitten is purring, and my socks are almost dry, but it's still absolutely pouring rain.

4:13 p.m.

Good news—it's finally stopped storming, and if I run fast, Ash might still be waiting at the **Academy**.

5:41 p.m. Home

Just back from checking out MY NEW SCHOOL!

Unlike anything else I've seen in this place, the **Academy** is mega-modern, with lots of glass and steel and upbeat quotes about excellence stuck everywhere:

Believe To Achieve

In It For The Win

We Love League Tables, etc. etc. etc.

There are all-weather sports pitches that look AMAZING, too! It's not as big as the high school I'd have gone to if we hadn't moved, but it's still sort of scary, especially because the year's already started.

I told Ash I was nervous, and he said he'd introduce me to all his friends. "You'll like it! It's just an ordinary school," he said, as if that were something to be very proud of.

I wanted to go and see the *other* school—the one named the School of Extraordinary Arts that I'd heard Mrs. Namdar talking about—but Ash said we didn't have time because it's in the forest and it was getting late. It's true that the forest is very DARK and DEEP and TANGLY, but it's literally at the end of our yards, and it's not that late. I don't think that was Ash's only reason for not giving me a tour. He says the Academy is the only "proper" school here and that I should forget about the other one. I don't know what he meant by that—maybe the schools have an epic rivalry.

On the way home, I saw two more orange bubble cars with what looked like bright purple sparks coming out of their exhausts. Ash just shrugged and said I'd get used to it.

Odd.

7:32 p.m.

Dad said Ash could stay for dinner, but Ash had to go home and do his homework. It was probably for the best because tonight's menu was burned sausages with a side of sandwich cookies. Dad might know everything there is to know about thunder-snow, but he is a *disaster* in the kitchen.

Must add "Learn to cook" to my list of **Things I Will ACHIEVE This Year Now That I Have No Friends Only One Friend.**

SATURDAY SEPTEMBER 18

9:00 p.m. Home

Missed a few days, but only because I ~~lost misplaced~~ secured my diary in the bread box.

Anyway, the only interesting thing that has happened to me in the last four days has been BAD.

I found out that I am NOT going to the **Academy**. I'm going to the OTHER school—the Extraordinary one stuck in the forest! And it's totally Dad's fault. All he had to do was register me at the library and he messed it up—he was so busy obsessing about peculiar precipitation* that he wrote my name in the *wrong book*.

"I'm sure the School of Extraordinary Arts is just as good," was what he said when he finally summoned up

---

*Or funny rain as normal people call it.

the courage to tell me what he'd done. "It'll be *fine*."

"But I don't even have ONE friend there," I wailed.

"You'll make friends." Dad made it sound like the easiest thing in the world. "And, until you do, you'll have more time for math!" He laughed. I didn't. Instead, I ~~demanded~~ asked nicely that he UNregister me ASAP.

But although he said he was sorry about a hundred times and looked as sheepish as an actual sheep *and* gave me the last fluffmallow in the house, apparently school transfers are tricky and the best he could do was promise to *try*. "But give it a good shot first, Bea," he said hopefully. "Maybe it's fate...."

It's not FATE—it's a

DISASTER.

Maybe he'll feel so guilty he'll buy me a puppy.

SUNDAY SEPTEMBER 19 (GOING-TO-NEW-SCHOOL EVE!)

11:43 p.m. Home

I'm not asleep. Well, *obviously* I'm not because otherwise I couldn't be writing this, but more to the point, I'm too ~~scared~~ EXCITED to sleep. Okay, I am a tiny bit scared, but that's because Ash came over earlier and went on and on in a not-at-all-reassuring way about how the *extraordinary* thing about the School of Extraordinary Arts was how WEIRD it was. I said it was just school and how strange could it be? And he said, "Have you seen the uniform?" and laugh-snorted so hard some of the Coke he was drinking came out of his nose.

Of course I've seen the uniform. I'm looking at it

right now—freshly ironed (Dad only burned through the fabric once) and folded up on the stool at the bottom of my bed. I don't hate it, but it's ... *distinctive*.

A purple pinafore so dark it looks almost black

A gold silk tie with fat black diagonal stripes

A white shirt with a starched collar - and, in my case, one very badly burned cuff

Socks with bright gold-and-pink stripes (the sixth grade colors)

And - this is the part I really do like - instead of a blazer we have a short, flippy cape - midnight-purple lined in gold silk with a long hood and little tassels that tie at the neck

Ash might think it's HILARIOUS, but he has a robe covered in robots so I don't see why he's suddenly the authority on fashion.

MONDAY SEPTEMBER 20 (UGHHHHHHHH!)

12:06 a.m. Home

TODAY'S THE DAY! I should probably go to sleep now.

1:56 a.m.

I should definitely go to sleep now....

What *are* Extraordinary Arts? I wish I were better at drawing.

2:12 a.m.

Just woke up, panicking that I'd overslept.

7:56 a.m.

How could Dad let me oversleep?!

8:13 a.m.

I don't know why I was up half the night worrying about school. I should have been worrying about BREAKFAST. How can my dad be a scientist and not know the difference between salt and sugar? That's the kind of detail that makes all the difference with Good Luck Pancakes.

I tell him they're YUMMY and manage to eat almost a whole one so as not to hurt his feelings. He says, "I'm sure you'll be FINE!" about a hundred times so I don't think he's *that* sure. "You'll find your feet in no time," he promises.

Talking of feet, the striped socks look even brighter this morning. I'm basically *glowing* from the knees down. Then Dad asked me if I was okay walking to school on my own on the first day and I said of course I was because I knew he had an important meeting with a snowflake specialist from Greenland, and anyway all I had to do was follow the path that started at the end of our yard. I'd be *fine*. Probably.

"I KNOW everything will go really well today," says Dad. Mmm, well, I guess it can't get worse than the pancakes.

9:09 a.m. School

I was WRONG.

I haven't even been to class and I'm already sitting outside the principal's office.

I think it might be because I squashed her cat.

I didn't mean to, *obviously*. I'm not EVIL, and it wasn't because I prefer dogs (which is something I'm going to have to keep quiet about because of Little Spellshire being the Cat Capital of the United States and possibly the world). It was a **Very Unfortunate Accident** and mostly the broom's fault.

I was already running late because of the whole sleeping in and suffering-through-the-pancakes thing and I was barely five minutes down the forest path when it suddenly got super foggy and I'd have gotten lost if I hadn't spotted a pair of capes flashing gold through the trees ahead. I followed them at double speed past a swampy green pond, through a brambly patch, and out into a clearing. The fog lifted as suddenly as it had dropped, and I could see the school! It had tall, twisty chimneys and gray turrets like a castle! Huge iron gates were propped open by what looked like big PUMPKINS, and more caped students in groups of twos and threes were streaming through.

Eeeek! I was only halfway up the driveway when the loudest bell I'd ever heard shook one of the towers. I was pretty sure that meant I was LATE. I made a run for it, and if someone hadn't *left a broom right in the doorway*, I might have made it all the way to registration without a DISASTER.

But they *did* and I *didn't*.

Obviously, I tripped over it and skidded across the marble entrance hall.

"LOOK OUT!" someone yelled—I was heading straight for the lady at the front desk! I quickly swerved and landed instead with a terrible **thump** on something *soft* ... that *yowled*....

I was too scared to look.

There was a hissing noise like air escaping out of a balloon and then SILENCE (broken only by nervous giggles and gasps from the *audience* of other students). But after a few seconds of extreme and worrying FLATNESS, the little black cat— because that's what I'd landed on—sort of puffed back into three dimensions, got up, gave me a hard stare, and walked away with its tail in the air.

Phew! There was a smattering of applause. But the receptionist (who was *extremely* old and looked a bit like my grandpa's tortoise if it had been wearing a black frilly dress) was NOT HAPPY.

"That's all this school needs," she said. "Another one."

"Another what, Mrs. Slater?" asked a boy in a cloak that was about ten sizes too big.

"*Pupil,*" she replied in the sort of tone other people would use for words like "black widow spider" or

"plague." She came out from behind the desk
to check that I, no, that the BROOM was okay.
"Too many children," she muttered darkly,
placing it in a very large coat closet full of other
brooms. So many brooms! I guess it must be hard
to keep this place clean—even the entrance hall
was three stories high with a big fireplace and the
sort of cobweb-decorated staircase that looked
like it belonged in a ghost story.

I was trying to distract myself from the crisis-
at-hand with a little daydream of sliding down the
wiggly banisters when a tall girl about my age,
wearing the neatest sports uniform I've ever seen
in my life, said snippily that, "Only a **toadbrain**
wouldn't jump over a broom." Then she informed me
that I'd *assaulted* the *principal's* cat and *now I'd be
in for it* and laughed. And, sure enough, two minutes
later Mrs. Slater was telling a scary senior to show
me to the principal's office....

So here I am.

In for it.

9:29 a.m.

Well, that was a lot better than I was expecting. Turns out Ms. Sparks, the principal, had only sent for me because she wanted to say hello on my first day! She said it must be very intimidating for someone like me to come to a school like this. I said—without specifically mentioning the squashing-her-pet thing—that I'd certainly had a rocky start.

"We can't have that," she said, all twinkly, and gave me a cookie so of course I felt guilty and confessed. But she just laughed and told me not to worry about Zephyr because there was "more to her than meets the eye." And the cat, who'd been staring at me in a very judgy way from the top of a bookcase full of ancient books, leaped down and settled smugly on her owner's shoulder.

It was a good thing I hadn't landed on Stan, said Ms. Sparks, because he had a tendency to be in the wrong place at the wrong time and was quite squishable. I asked her who Stan was, but she just said I'd meet him very soon.

"I was surprised to see your name on our list," she went on, "but then I remembered meeting your father in the butcher shop and having a most interesting conversation about the effect of thunderstorms on cheese and I expect that explains it." That explained nothing, but it did sound very like Dad.

Ms. Sparks asked me lots of questions like, what was my favorite subject? (PE) and did I enjoy homework? ("Love it!" I fibbed). Then she told me I mustn't worry too much about my grandparents not having gone to this school—which was an odd thing to say because they've never left Milton Keynes.

"Whatever you might imagine, Bea, and no matter what some people want to believe," she said, "it's not all inherited, you know. No student walks in here knowing it all, no matter who their ancestors are, and, if you ask me, there's not much knowledge worth acquiring that doesn't take a good deal of hard work. No one's born excellent at baking, are they?"

Judging from my last attempt to make brownies, probably not.

"And no one's born knowing their eight times table, are they?"

DEFINITELY not.

"HARD WORK AND FOCUS and you'll be flying in no time! Flying—hahaha! But remember: Don't tell a soul. Those of us who know, *know* and those of them who don't, *can't.*"

I nodded enthusiastically, but it was all very confusing.

"Excellent!" she said. "I'm glad we understand each other." I wasn't sure what to say because I did NOT understand her, so I admired her dress, which was covered in glittery gold stars, and she gave me another cookie. Then she told me to wait right there while she went to get it for me— whatever "it" was.

9:41 a.m.

I'm back outside the principal's office and I am
SHOOK.

Ash was right. This place IS weird. Very, *extremely*,
EXTRAORDINARILY WEIRD.

"It" was a *wand*.

A WAND.

A real ... actual ...

WAND.

For ME.

I wouldn't have known that's what it was because
at first glance it looked a bit like a bumpy chopstick,
but Ms. Sparks was VERY insistent that it WAS a wand
and she doesn't seem like the sort of principal to joke
about that kind of thing. Also, when I fell over in shock,
she pulled out *her* wand and *spelled me upright
again*!

"See!" she said with a grin.

I might be back on my feet, but my head's spinning
and I'm very NERVOUS and maybe I shouldn't be
writing any of this down because Ms. Sparks said

I wasn't to tell ANYONE. But she's ducked back into her office to print me out a schedule so she can't see me, and anyway, do diaries even count? Maybe I could write in secret code?

7**HƆS HƆꞱ*M *ꓭ W* 1

Maybe not. For now, I'll just have to make sure nobody reads this. EVER. Anyway, I can't write any more because Ms. Sparks is coming back and she's going to take me to my first class—physics.

Did I say? I am in a state of **SHOCK**.

12:43 p.m.

It's only lunchtime but I'm hiding in a broom coat closet with a frog.

A LOT has happened.

"You'll have a head start," Ms. Sparks had said on the way to the physics classroom. "What with your father being a scientist."

I didn't tell her I'd inherited Dad's awkwardness, but not his good-at-science-y-ness.

"Most of physics is quite straightforward, isn't it? What goes up must come down," she said, then she opened a classroom door, shouted "Good luck!" and *abandoned* me.

It was CHAOS.

I was staring into a big room with about twenty students sitting at desks while one student was being shouted at by a teacher to *get down*. So far, so ordinary, except that ... *the desks were at least three feet off the ground*! And that seemed to be the part of the lesson that was going WELL because the student everyone was shouting at was not just twice as high up as the others: He was *upside down* with his hair dripping some sort of blue goo onto the students below.

"Woo-hoo! I'm JUGGLING!" he yelled. "*No hands!*" And I have to admit what that boy could do upside down with five tennis balls and one frog was pretty amazing!

Suddenly upside-down boy saw me looking, said, "Cat Girl?," lost concentration, and he, the desk, the balls, and the frog all lurched alarmingly downward! I let out a shriek just as the teacher grabbed something off his desk that looked very much like my wand, muttered something I didn't catch, and without anyone else seeming to move a finger, the boy and everything else turned the right way up again before floating gently to the ground.

"If you try that again, Puck Berry," said the teacher, glaring at the boy, "it's detention. And I'll take Stan, thank you very much." He scooped up the sad-looking frog and marched in my direction.

By the time he got to me, he was all smiley, holding out his hand and introducing himself as Mr. Muddy. He looked like a physics teacher should, in a mismatched three-piece suit and a flowing white robe that I think was the witch equivalent of a lab coat.

"Everyone," Mr. Muddy said as he popped Stan-the-frog on his head and clapped his hands. "Meet Bea Black—New Girl! Haven't had one of those in forever! *Such fun!*"

Twenty pairs of eyes swiveled in my direction.

"Introductions, everyone!" ordered Mr. Muddy and immediately, on every desk, a name appeared scrawled in different handwriting and scrawled in *my* handwriting on the only empty desk in the room was MY name!

Even though I was almost falling over with nerves, I could appreciate that this trick was not only useful but very cool. My place was in between a girl with very curly hair who—I peeked at her desk—was named Winnie and ... *oh, no*, scary-sports-girl-who'd-called-me-a-**TOADBRAIN**, Blair. Mr. Muddy made her move her cape off my chair, which she did EXTREMELY slowly and with maximum side-eye. Then, as I was awkwardly hesitating, the chair shot out, my bottom sort of *attached* itself to the seat like it was on magnets, and with a **WHOOSH** I was tucked in!

"Ooopsy!" I said.

"Who says 'ooopsy'?" Blair asked Hunter, the boy sitting in front of her.

"Lame," he muttered. (He had a point: I'd never said that before in my life!)

"Oooopsy!" I found myself saying again as the chair rearranged me a little closer to the desk. Blair and Hunter and Izzi—the girl sitting on the other side of Blair—all snickered.

"Wands out!" Before I even had time to get to my schoolbag, my wand (MY WAND?!) leaped into my hand. "Levitation one-o-one," called out Mr. Muddy to a chorus of groans. "Every witch's entry-level skill—let's see what Bea can do."

What *could* Bea do? I ransacked my brain. Nope, not a single science fact that had anything to do with levitation (I wasn't even sure I knew what the word meant).

"Come on!" he encouraged me. "Use your wand skills—get something in the air."

All eyes were on me. Even my wand curled back like a cat's tail and *looked at me*.

"Just point it at something and, you know, tell it to go UP," muttered Winnie. As advice went, it was a bit vague, but it was all I had. I shook the wand back into a straight line and pointed it at a notebook that was lying on my desk.... Surprise, surprise, nothing happened. In the meantime, everyone else was getting bored and all around me random objects—textbooks, fluffy key rings, pens, a banana—were floating off desks and into the air. It was very distracting.

"Come on, Bea-Black-New-Girl!" Mr. Muddy fist-pumped the air in encouragement. *Oh, dear.*

"Let your wand know who's boss," Winnie directed in a loud whisper.

I was not feeling boss-vibes, but I had to do something, so I desperately *willed* the wand to do as it was told. *Wait* ... I could feel something happening. It was a sort of quivering, like a sneeze that wouldn't happen. *Pleeeease*, I begged it, *pleeeease*. Finally, with a cross little jerk, it spat out a crackle of sparks, which on the upside was VERY SURPRISING AND MAGICAL, but on the downside....

"Fire!" yelled Puck.

He was not wrong. Not only was my face AFLAME with embarrassment, one of the flying textbooks had caught fire and was zooming around the classroom.

"Fire!" yelled student after student, ducking out of the way. There were now at least five flaming books and a strong smell of burning banana.

Mr. Muddy swooshed his wand, said something I didn't understand ... and suddenly, it was RAINING!

The fires were out, but I was mortified. I was also quite damp. I'd have run away except I didn't think my chair would let me.

"Don't worry," said Winnie, toweling her hair with her cloak, "nerves always mess up magic. On my first day, I set fire to my eyebrows." I wasn't sure I believed her, but at least she was talking to me—most of the other students were giving me judgy looks as they collected their stuff.

I was the last one to leave the classroom, and Mr. Muddy (who, it turned out, was the sixth grade advisor) had one last "gift for me." "Here, I'm putting you on Stan duty until further notice." And before I had time to say anything, my hands were full of clammy FROG. "I know he doesn't seem like much, but he's quite a *consoling* frog."

Stan gave me a look that was something close to DESPAIR.

Anyway, longest diary entry EVER, but now you* know why I'm ~~hiding away~~ enjoying some alone-with-a-frog time while everyone else has lunch.

1:11 p.m.

Stan's started making a funny noise, more like a **bark** than a **croak**. Maybe he's hungry. What do frogs eat? Clearly, nothing in my lunch box. Please tell me it's not ALIVE things.

2:48 p.m.

Just got out of English.

When I say "English," what I mean is Incantations and the Language of Spells.

"It's not always enough just to wave your wand

---

* Have become one of those peculiar people who talk to their diaries.

at something," said Madam Binx, plucking a cobweb off the giant Venus flytrap sitting on her desk and picking up a little gold watering can. "That might work for basic UP-DOWN stuff like *levitation,* but for something more specific and creative, you need to strengthen the spell with the right WORDS." Everyone except me nodded, as if she were making perfect sense. "Who can give me an example of something that makes word spells stronger?"

"Rhymes!" Blair called out.

"Good answer!" replied Madam Binx, carefully replacing the cobweb on the freshly watered plant. "Now which one of you witches is going to come up with an original rhyming spell to start us off?" She was wasting her time looking at me. "Ordinary English will do."

"*Onto shelves and into nooks!*" yelled a girl in the front row, pointing her wand at a HUGE, tottering pile of textbooks in the corner. "*With this spell, I clean up these BOOKS!*"

I ducked as a heavy pink volume flew past my ear

to land on the shelf behind me. *Ahhhhhhhh*, and again! In seconds, the pile was gone, all the books were back in their places, and everyone (except the student who hadn't dodged in time and now had a bloody nose) was clapping. I clapped, too, but very quietly because I didn't want to draw attention to myself.

"Excellent work, Amara," said Madam Binx approvingly, and with a single flick, a gold star swooshed out the end of her wand and hovered above the girl's head for a moment before exploding into a little shower of sparks and one gold-wrapped candy that landed perfectly in her outstretched hand! "Okay, *focus-pocus*, class. I want each of you to come up with at least three words that rhyme with each of these." Madam Binx turned back to the old-fashioned blackboard and wrote:

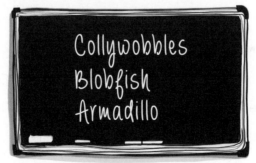

Collywobbles
Blobfish
Armadillo

Then she put down her pen, picked up her wand, and with a "*Snip-snip-SNAP, feed my flyTRAP*," magicked up a cloud of sparkly rainbow flying things for her pet plant!

I watched a twinkly blue bug land on the end of my pen and dissolve in a puff and ~~tried~~ FAILED to come up with something that rhymed with ARMADILLO. *Pocus-focus*, it was going to take more than some magic rhymes to calm me down today.

Polly-waffles?
Molly-coddles??
Slobwish?
Frogsquish??
Caterpillow???

2:50 p.m.
According to Winnie Ross,* frogs eat FROG FOOD— available from Mrs. Slater at the front office. If I have any sense, she said, I won't ask what that is.

* Or Winnie Boss as Hunter calls her (I don't think he's being friendly).

2:51 p.m.

The history teacher is out sick. Instead, "for a treat" (haha), Mr. Muddy is going to give us an extra lesson in physics. *Noooooooo....*

3:09 p.m.

How long can I make this bathroom break last?

3:13 p.m.

When will this day end?

6:20 p.m. Home

Dad's been home for exactly seven minutes (okay, eight now) and he hasn't stopped quizzing me on my day. "What are the teachers like? Did you meet the principal? Did you do well in class?" And, of course, the killer question, "Have you made any friends?"

I could barely speak after the day I'd had, but I managed to answer: "Yes, the teachers were okay," "Yes, the principal was really nice but also a bit ... *unusual,*" *shrug* (because admitting that the only thing I'd managed to do was set the classroom on fire wasn't an option) and *SHRUG* (because I didn't want to tell him I hadn't made any friends because they all think I'm a **TOADBRAIN**).

Then Dad got all grumpy about me being "*uncommunicative*" and said he'd never have bought me a diary if he'd known I was going to spend more time "talking to it" than him, so I showed him my COMPLETELY NORMAL schedule.

Schedule: Sixth grade (Form Advisor: Mr. Muddy)
Student Name: BEA BLACK

Time	Monday	Tuesday	Wednesday	Thursday	Friday
09:00–09:15	Registration	Registration	Registration	Registration	Registration
09:20–10:00	Physics	Art	Chem/Biology	Chem/Biology	PE
10:05–10:50	Physics	Art	Math	Zoology	PE
10:55–11:15	Break	Break	Break	Break	Break
11:20–12:00	Physics	Math	English	Math	Math
12:05–1:05	Lunch	Lunch	Lunch	Lunch	Lunch
1:10–1:55	PD	PD	Whole School Assembly	PD	PD
2:00–2:45	English	English	Physics	History	Friday Lecture
2:50–3:30	History	Chem/Biology	Physics	English	Physics

NOTHING TO SEE HERE ↗

Dad asked me what PD (Personal Development) was, so I told him it was basically free time (or what Mr. Muddy had named "time to let your imagination go wild").

"Excellent, excellent!" said Dad, who very much approved of free time—but then I didn't tell him I spent it all in a coat closet with a FROG. "And so much physics!" He beamed.

8:02 p.m.

Dad might be optimistic, but he's not clueless, and it didn't take him long to go back to asking me if I was *sure* everything was okay. Everything was FINE, I ~~lied~~ said, but when we were washing dishes, I reminded him of his promise to see if I could transfer to the **Academy**. He said he would, but then started talking to me in a Concerned-Parent Voice about Giving Things A Chance and Facing New Challenges, so I fled to bed.

NEW CHALLENGES?!

He has no idea.

9:15 p.m.

Ash is waving at me from his bedroom window.

"How. Did. It. Go?" he mouthed.

"A-MA-ZING," I mouthed back because that wasn't exactly a lie.

He opened the window and bellowed across, "Was it ... EXTRAORDINARY?" And then he snorted like he'd said something very funny. He has no idea.

I'm not going to open my window because I'm not really in the mood to chat.

I'm not even in the mood to write this **TOP-SECRET** diary entry. Which reminds me: Must add "Learn to write in code" to my list of **Things I Will ACHIEVE This Year Now That I Have ~~No Friends~~ Only One Friend (and a frog).**

9:37 p.m.
C*D25 SI 4*RD
TERCES TON YREV??
EQFH HU JCTF!!

10:10 p.m.
Abandoned attempts to learn code and spent an
hour looking for a mega-safe hiding place for this

diary, but in the end have settled
on my sock drawer. You could hide
anything in there—it's very messy.
My wand is still in my schoolbag
because I'm too ~~scared~~ sensible
to take it out. To be on the safe
side, I've put the bag in my
wardrobe and rammed a
chair against the door.
Should be FINE.

TUESDAY SEPTEMBER 21

1:45 a.m. Home

Woke up sweating. I had this *terrifying* nightmare that I'd gone to a school full of WITCHES and FROGS.

1:46 a.m.

Just checked the wardrobe. There *is* actually *a wand* in my schoolbag. So not a dream then....

8:13 a.m.

(STILL Tuesday—I've been awake for hours.)

Dad is feeling guilty because there are no eggs in the house, and according to an article he read yesterday in *Science Today*, my education is doomed unless I *"Go to School on an Egg."* I don't think breakfast is my biggest problem. Anyway, it's not his fault; he was distracted by a Very Surprising MINI-TORNADO outside **Spellshire's Sensible Store** yesterday and came home with nothing more than one very large box of pasta, three onions, and a container of raspberries.

On the upside, raspberries for breakfast.

On the downside, no packed lunch. *Wait!* That might be an upside, too....

11:14 a.m. School

Art is EXTRA-extraordinary at this school! Mr. Zicasso wanted us all to "let our inner Da Vinciwick out." This was very tricky for me because I didn't know who or what Da Vinciwick *is*, but it involved a LOT of paint flying around the classroom, and Puck was sent outside to stand in the hallway for drawing a big purple bat on Fabi's cloak. But no time to write about it all now, because since I don't know how to SPELL my uniform clean like everyone else seems to, I've had to spend the entire break in the bathrooms trying to scrub out the paint.

Stan is sulking—possibly because he is now more of a pink-and-blue frog than a muddy-green one. I tried telling him it was a good look, but he ignored me.

12:06 p.m.

Very confused. I've just come out of math and there was something strange going on.

More to the point, there *wasn't* anything strange going on.

We just sat there in near-silence and mastered fractions* under the stern gaze of Mr. Smith, who was wearing a gray suit with a not-even-striped tie.

Where's magic when you need it?

12:10 p.m.

No packed lunch means I'm going to have to brave

---

*I did NOT master fractions.

SCHOOL LUNCH, and I'd rather face an army of flaming dragons (which, the way things are going, will probably be next week's challenge).

Obviously, it's not the actual *lunch* that's worrying me. I'm STARVING. But it's a lot easier to hide the fact I don't have any friends when I'm sitting in a coat closet with Stan, rather than sitting *on my own* at lunch with *no one to talk to*. I'm trying to look really busy writing this in the line to go into the lunchroom so nobody notices me. Maybe I could just ask a passing witch to invisibility spell me?

NOT Puck.

12:21 p.m.

Except ... *mmmmmm*, something smells good.

12:23 p.m.
Sausages?

12:25 p.m.

Winnie has come to tell me where to get my tray
and plastic fork and spoon—apparently, she's lunch
monitor (she's monitor of just about everything) and ...
she's asked me to come and sit with her and Puck and
Fabi and Amara!

I think this is *good*!

12:28 p.m.

Wow, this is NOT your average school lunchroom.
It's a huge room with wood-paneled walls dotted with
old-fashioned portraits of important-looking people
in black capes, and up front, laid out on a long, carved
high table, there's literally a BANQUET! There are big,
steaming ~~pots~~ cauldrons of some sort of stew and—
my nose never lies—fat, sizzling *sausages* are cooking
over a real open fire. And the pudding table is even
better, with trifles almost as tall as me, and CAKES,
so many cakes! It's like Christmas but better because
Dad's not cooking.

Things are finally looking up.

1:19 p.m.

Things are no longer looking up.

I'd ~~greedily~~ enthusiastically heaped my plate with sausages (and some sprouts because the cook—who they all named Sir and who clearly wasn't someone to be argued with—had insisted) and squeezed on to the bench between Puck and Winnie, with Stan on my knee. Amara was having an argument across the table with Fabi about which of them should be captain of some PE team.

"Soccer?" I asked hopefully.

Fabi laughed and shook his head and when I asked what they did play—basketball? Baseball? (anything with a ball would be fine by me)—he just grinned and said I'd find out. Then they started placing bets on who would score the most goals that year.

"It won't be either of you," said Winnie dismissively. "Blair always scores the most."

I said she must be really good at sports and they all said yes, she was, and *very* COMPETITIVE. Cool. It didn't seem the moment to tell them I was very competitive, too, so I changed the subject and said the first thing that came into my head—that I hadn't known boys could be witches.

Winnie was horrified. "That's so SEXIST," she said.

"And OLD-FASHIONED!" added Amara disapprovingly.

"But aren't boys *wizards*?" I plowed on.

There was a sharp intake of breath.

"Wizards are something else *entirely*," said Puck.

They *were*? I had so many questions, but they

were all looking at me like they couldn't believe I didn't know what they were talking about, so I lost my nerve and focused on my sausages.

"Dig in," said Winnie encouragingly, so I took an enormous bite....

BLLLEEUUGH!

I *spat out* what was left in my mouth with such a lurch of disgust that Stan shot off my knee and flew halfway across the room. Oh, no! All the witch students and one very large witch cook were staring at me.

"*Rude!*" loud-whispered Hunter from the next table. He had a point. I don't normally SPIT.

"B-but it tastes like—" I spluttered.

"Yes?" Scary Witch Cook was looming over our table like Dracula over a coffin. "*What* does it taste like?"

Um, not like any sausage I'd ever tasted. The closest I could get was inside-of-a-dog-basket-with-a-sprinkling-of-gherkin.

"It t-tastes s-surprising, S-Sir," I stuttered.

Blair, who was sitting next to Hunter, rolled her

eyes and chipped in with, "She's not used to OUR food, I suppose." She wasn't the only student tutting, though—turns out witches, as a bunch, are a bit *judgmental*. Even Winnie, handing Stan back to me, looked disappointed. (Stan looked pretty horrified, too, but maybe that was because he'd just been catapulted across the room and had landed on a teacher.)

Mr. Scary Cook folded his arms across his huge chest and glared down at me. "Eat up," he said.

Everyone else was chomping away happily enough— maybe I'd just gotten a weird part. Another look at Scary Cook persuaded me I had no choice. I took a second mouthful.

EEEEEEUGH!

This time I was getting definite hints of blue-cheese-with-cat-food. Little beads of sweat were breaking out on my forehead as I chewed.

"Well?" asked Scary Cook.

"D-Delicious," I managed, bright red with the effort of not spitting it out. What I would have given for one of Dad's salty pancakes. In the end, the only thing on my plate that was edible were the SPROUTS because they tasted like, well, *sprouts*. Things are bad when that's a win.

I think Winnie regretted asking me to sit at their table. Turns out witches are not just *judgy* but very easily OFFENDED.

3:01 p.m.

So chemistry is POTIONS and I'm not even surprised anymore.

"What do you mean you haven't made a potion before?" asked Miss Lupo. Even after I'd explained I was new to Little Spellshire, she still couldn't get her head around it. "But surely you covered the basic concoctions at home?"

I had no idea what "basic concoctions" were, but she looked so worried that I nodded.

"Well, that's a relief!" she said. "Goodness knows what would happen if you started making potions without knowing the basics! Hahahahaha!"

I wasn't laughing because I was too busy worrying about when we were going to find out.

"Spells aren't only about waving your wand or saying the right words—whatever the other teachers might tell you," she said. "Sometimes only a potion will do, and that means learning about all the right ingredients and what to do with them."

Great. Another kind of magic for me to FAIL at.

Bear Breeches and Snapdragons, she wrote on the board, telling us to copy it in our notebooks. "Such an exciting combination!"

I'd ink-blotted my page so I tore it out, scrunched it up, and without thinking, lobbed it halfway across the classroom into the garbage can.

"Good shot!" called out Blair from right behind me, making me jump, and a second later not one but two balls of scrumpled paper flew over my head and landed perfectly in the basket.

That was a *great* shot ... but I could definitely do better. I was just about to attempt a TRIPLE when a voice said, "Bea Black and Blair Smith-Smythe! This is not a PE class." Miss Lupo was standing by my desk with a small, smoking cauldron in her hand. *Oops.*

"Now which one of you can tell me whether you would add one *tablespoon* or *half a teaspoon* of mucklespit to this recipe?"

Um ... not me.

Speaking of recipes, I'm so hungry I could eat a horse.

3:03 p.m.

Just seen a horse cantering past the window! Okay, maybe not *that* hungry, but really VERY hungry-starving indeed.

I swear I can still taste those sausages. **YUCK!**

6:40 p.m. Home

I ate every last mouthful of Dad's homemade mac 'n' cheese, even though he'd forgotten to put in any cheese. "Yum!" I said.

He looked surprised.

"Can I have a second helping?"

He almost fell off his chair. "That school is doing wonders for your appetite, Bea."

Dad looks tired. His book on *Understanding Little Spellshire's Most Peculiar Microclimate* is apparently "going nowhere." I know the feeling. My math homework is also going nowhere, unfortunately.

The unicorns at Zany Zoo are fed seven-tenths of a barrel of fluffmallows every day. The centaurs are fed half as many fluffmallows as the unicorns. How many barrels of fluffmallows are the centaurs fed in a week?

Seriously? All I know is that unicorns and centaurs should NOT be in a zoo.

I think the main reason Dad's upset is because

ALMOST

I'm not telling him anything. I used to talk to him about everything that happened at my last school. "But how is it *really* going?" he keeps asking, peering at me like I'm a particularly worrying cloud. I want to say that the only way it could be going *worse* would be if my Extraordinary School turned into an Extraordinary Boarding School, but instead I just mutter that I'm not sure I *fit in*.

"But it's good to stand out!" Dad says and I DESPAIR.

7:21 p.m.

I waited until we were washing the dishes and then asked Dad if he'd had any luck getting me transferred to the **Academy**. He looked guilty and told me to "leave it with him." That means he's forgotten.

I'm going to stick Post-it note reminders all over the house until he sorts this out.

8:11 p.m.

Ash came over and we watched an old movie about a scientist who'd shrunk his kids. Ash (who takes science very seriously) thought the plot was ridiculous, but I thought it was the sanest thing I'd seen all day.

Afterward, Ash asked me tons of questions about school and got all grumpy when I wouldn't/*couldn't* answer. Then he told me the **Academy** was having a **Halloween** soccer match and I am so jealous I could SCREAM.

9:56 p.m.

I wonder what makes wizards different from witches?

WEDNESDAY SEPTEMBER 22

10:32 a.m. School

Math. Still haven't figured it out. When will the magic kick in?

I hope Dad remembered to do something about GETTING ME OUT OF HERE.

12:37 p.m.

Packed lunch in the broom coat closet with Stan again. I've never had raisin-and-tomato sandwiches before, but they're surprisingly okay. I wish I had some fluffmallows.

People keep saying words I don't understand, so I think I'll go to the library now. I've got a long list of things I need to look up.

12:57 p.m.

> [Extract from English Dictionary:]
>
> **Levitation,** *noun*
>
> The act of rising, or causing something to rise
> and hover in the air, typically by means of
> supposed magical powers.

What this library's missing is a helpful introductory manual on how to be a witch. Shame.

1:56 p.m.

Survived my first assembly in the **Great Hall** (a room so ridiculously HUGE and GRAND it makes the lunchroom look ordinary), despite Ms. Sparks pointing me out to the whole SCHOOL as the NEW GIRL. "Make sure you all give her an Extraordinary welcome!" she said.

I overheard Izzi mutter, "We sure will," to Blair, who

was sitting next to her.

A couple of eighth graders who'd been sitting at the next table at lunch yesterday were pointing me out to their friends, and I'd probably have burst with embarrassment there and then if it hadn't been for Ms. Sparks's next announcement—the Halloween Costume Ball would take place on, *wait for it* ... HALLOWEEN. There was so much cheering I had to cover Stan's little ears.

"I expect everyone to make a splendid effort with their costumes this year," bellowed the principal. "Applications for the Junior Ball Committee are to be made in writing to my office, and if you want to have a chance of being crowned this year's Queen or King of Mischief (*more cheering*), write your name on a slip of paper and drop it into the cauldron by Mrs. Slater's desk no later than dismissal time this Friday!" The hall just about exploded with excitement. I was surprised the noise didn't bring down the great, cow-sized, glittering chandelier that was hanging above our heads.

No one was talking about the New Girl anymore.

2:01 p.m.

I wonder what the **Queen or King of Mischief** does?

3:32 p.m.

Why are witches so obsessed with making things go
up in the air? Especially things that really
should NOT go up.

Like frogs.

Or ME. Hunter might have
thought it was *hilarious* to
spell me from the bottom of
the Grand Staircase to the top,
but I didn't.

I am ~~TROMA TRAUMMATIZED~~
SHOOK.

8:15 p.m. Home

Still too shook to write anything down, so maybe I'll
start on my physics homework.

Levitate three books of varied sizes—does an increased number of pages increase the difficulty of levitation? Record your results.

Or maybe I'll just lie on my bed and feel sorry for myself instead.

THURSDAY SEPTEMBER 23

DAD TO DO URGENTLY, BEFORE HALLOWEEN!!!

Arrange for Bea to MOVE SCHOOLS

FRIDAY SEPTEMBER 24

8:52 a.m. School

It's PE today. *Finally*, a lesson where I'll know
what I'm doing. I've eaten three bananas for
breakfast and I'm ready for anything.

   New day, new me.

   Upbeat-Bea-Me.

11:00 a.m.

I did NOT know what I was doing.

   Everything seemed ordinary enough to start.
I practically bounced out to the pitch in my new
purple sports uniform with my old sneakers on.
Okay, so it might take some time to get picked for a
team, but this was a challenge I was up for.

The PE coach, Ms. Celery, looked normal—not a flowing cape in sight, just a plain tracksuit and a sideways baseball cap with WINNER written on it. "Snoozers are LOSERS!" she roared, sounding exactly like my last PE teacher. Happy days! "Come over here and collect your broomsticks."

And right there and then my upbeat mood melted away faster than a chocolate ice-cream cone in a heatwave.

BROOMSTICKS.

Last time I'd encountered a broom, it hadn't turned out well, and the stuff I knew now that I hadn't known then wasn't making me any more confident.

"Is ... there ... flying involved?" I asked.

Ms. Celery looked at me like I was a bug (and she was one of those peculiar people who doesn't like bugs) and said, "*Obviously.*"

Great. So, instead of worrying about whether I'd get picked for a team, I should have been worrying about whether I might DIE.

"My skills are more *on the ground*—" I began, but before I could tell her just how good I was at dribbling, tackling, and passing, she snapped at me to leave "that frog" in the locker room and get my BUTT out on the pitch. "MOVE IT, NEW GIRL!"

So I did, and a minute later I was standing in front of her, minus Stan, *quaking*.

"Do you know the rules of **GO**?" she barked.

Go? I'd have GONE *anywhere* at this point as long as it was on foot. I shook my head, and she started shouting instructions at me so fast my head spun.

"Okay, no time for the finer points of the game, just remember the BASICS—ten players a side, nine of them—the **GOers**—out on the pitch, the other one—the Sweep—indoors. The sole aim for the **GOers** is to get the ball into the goal using only their hands or the broom. Simple, right?" *Posssssibly* ... but, then again, probably not.

"Where are the goals?" I asked because the not-so-normal thing about the pitch (other than the two cats chilling in the middle) was that there didn't seem to be any.

"There," she said, pointing up.

"Where?" All I could see were the battlements of the school roofs and the twisty chimneys.

"*There.* To score you have to hit the ball down the chimney. *The Great* Chimney." Ms. Celery jabbed her finger at the tallest, curliest one and told me it was a foul if the ball went down another one. So there really was ZERO chance of staying on the ground then? She juggled a ball the shape and color of an orange and looked me up and down. "You, I think, are a Dodo." *Rude!*

"Try out as a **GOer** today." And she handed me a neon-yellow bib and told me to put it on over my uniform.

Winnie, waving a clipboard, came over and told me she was the Sweep for the Dodos. "I have to sit near the fire in the entrance hall with the other team's Sweep," she explained. "If it's someone I like, we gossip, and if it's not I read my book."

Normally, I'd have thought that that sounded like the most boring sports position EVER, but right then, even if I'd had to read our math textbook from cover to cover, I'd have swapped with her. The Sweep's job was to record the score when the ball rolled out of the fireplace. I asked Winnie how she knew which team had scored and she told me the ball changed color. "Obviously."

Okkaaaaay.

Five minutes later, we were lined up, broomsticks in hand, in two witchy semicircles, the yellow DODOS and the bright red DRAGONS, facing each other on the pitch, and in the middle the cats (still chilling).

It was fast dawning on me that the game was about to start and *nobody had told me how to fly*. "Is it like riding a bike?" I whispered to Fabi, who was standing next to me.

"How would I know?" He shrugged, then peered at me and asked me if I was okay. "You look like you're going to be sick. Here...." He checked that Ms. Celery was too busy shouting at one of the Dragons to be watching, pulled a TINY pink striped sock out of his hood, and handed it to me. "My lucky sock," he explained. "It shrank in the wash, but it still works. You can borrow it." I had a feeling it was going to take more than a SOCK to keep me alive, but I stammered my thanks and stuck it in my pocket because I didn't know what else to do with it.

"And don't forget to be nice to your broom," Fabi called down.

Called down....

Everyone but me was now hovering feet up in the air!

"Hey! NEW GIRL!" bellowed Ms. Celery. "Get that broom up NOW!"

I swung my leg over the broom and it seemed to come ALIVE! Maybe it was the teacher who made it happen, maybe it was the lucky sock, but ... I was *UP*! Okay, I was wobbling and lurching, but I was *in the air*. Like a bird or a plane or an actual *witch*. And with Ms. Celery shouting at me to "GO! GO! GO!" I *went*.

"Don't look down!" yelled Blair, who was captaining the Dragons. "Whatever you do, Bea Black, don't look down. Ha!"

So, *of course*, I looked down....

AHHHHHHHHH!

I *crashed*. Over the next forty minutes, I *crashed* FIVE times, but ... I AM STILL ALIVE!!

That was not all. I also:

- threw the ball down the wrong chimney (one foul)
- threw the ball through the tenth grade common-room window (one foul and possibly worse to come when they find out)
- collided with Puck midair—total accident (one foul)
- collided with Blair midair four times—the first two times were a total accident (four fouls, *not fair*)
- broom-grabbed Hunter—*sort of* an accident (one foul)
- was the VICTIM of no less than SIX fouls awarded against the Dragons—ha!—four of them from

Blair, who is impressively aggressive in the air

- *wait for it ... SCORED a goal!!!!*

Final score:

DODOS: 33	DRAGONS: 32

Take that, Achievement List! It was WILD.

Riding a broomstick is NOTHING like riding a bike.

It's absolutely AMAZING.

11:05 a.m.

I was coming out of the locker room with Stan when I overheard Hunter telling Blair I was actually "quite good at **GO** for a **toadbrain**." I'd take that!

Blair said snippily that it wasn't fair to give me the credit because Ms. Celery had obviously given me a super-enchanted broom that a kindergartener could have stayed on and she'd still probably had to *spell me* the whole way through the game.

"You're just worried she's better than you," said Hunter.

Obviously, he was joking, but judging from her reply, Blair's not happy. Shame, because I was going to ask her how she managed to pull off a LOOP-THE-LOOP without falling off her broom. That's so going to the top of my **Things I Will ACHIEVE** list.

Look, maybe Blair's right and it was just the magic broom and beginner's luck, but *I don't care*. I've finally found something at the School of Extraordinary Arts I'm not HOPELESS at. Secretly feeling a tiny bit smug for the first time since I arrived in Little Spellshire.

11:15 a.m.

Nobody at this school knows how to ride a bike! Feeling SMUGGER.

12:02 p.m.

Just got out of math. Not feeling smug anymore.

3:35 p.m.

I will never feel smug again. Physics was TORTURE. Turns out that a) even when someone else has levitated something up in the air, I can't make it stay there (I honestly hadn't meant for the vase of flowers to drop on Mr. Muddy's toe) and b) the most important thing in wand-work is keeping your wand pointed at the thing or person you're enchanting (I *really* hadn't meant to set fire to his cloak).

"Magic on the loose," Mr. Muddy had said quite sternly, patting down his cloak, "even beginner's magic, can be very dangerous and unpredictable."

Oh, dear.

7:56 p.m. Home

I almost blabbed to Dad when I got home—not about physics and math and being a **toadbrain** *obviously*—but I was *bursting* to tell someone about my GOAL. It turns out it's as hard not telling him the good stuff as all the bad stuff, but as Ms. Sparks would say, "Those of us who know, *know* and those of them who don't, *can't*," so instead I told him about the Halloween Ball and then I wished I hadn't because he got VERY enthusiastic.

"Can I make you a costume?" he asked, and because he sounded like he really, really wanted to, I agreed.

I'm not even *ten percent* confident in Dad's needlework skills (the last thing he "sewed" for me was a ghost costume— AKA a sheet—and he forgot I'd need holes for my eyes), but WHAT DOES IT MATTER? By the time Halloween comes around, I'll have switched schools!

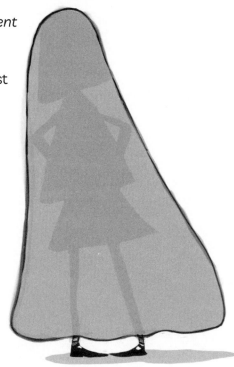

Pretty sure I won't have to worry about costumes at the **Academy**.

Cannot wait.

8:01 p.m.

Okay, I'll miss playing **GO**, but I won't miss anything else. I will especially not miss levitation and fractions and both kinds of spelling.

CANNOT WAIT.

SATURDAY SEPTEMBER 25

5:32 p.m. Home

Well, that was AWKWARD.

Went to Rhubarb & Custard with Ash to stock up on skullsquigglers and fluffmallows, and bumped into Amara and Fabi, who were buying out the shop's stock of purple twizzling sherbet. Ash stared at them like they were hungry tigers recently escaped from a zoo. To be fair, they did look a little different out of uniform. Amara was wearing a dress that seemed to be made out of leaves and had pulled her braids up into a topknot studded with hundreds of tiny glittery cats. Fabi had accessorized his silver FLARES with a squashed top hat.

Before I could ask Fabi where he got the hat, three

of Ash's friends from school crashed through the door, setting off the creaky old bell hanging above it. They stopped short when they saw who else was in the shop. Everyone stared at everyone else, and no one said a word. It was like some sort of military stand-off. The Extraordinaries on one side, the **Academy** kids (in jeans and hoodies) on the other. And I didn't know which group I belonged to! I *looked* like one of Ash's friends, I *was* one of Ash's friends, but also I was kind of, temporarily at least, an Extraordinary, and Fabi and Amara had never been mean to me. Also, I *really* liked Amara's dress.

In the end, I was so overwhelmed with awkwardness I accidentally spent all my allowance on lime gazugglers and they are DISGUSTING.

"Why don't the people who go to your school talk to the people who go to my—the *other* school?" I asked Ash on the way home.

He shrugged and muttered something about the people who went to Extraordinary not talking to *them* and being super-secretive.

"You don't mind me, though," I said and then pathetically asked, "do you?"

After a worrying pause, he said, "No." Then spoiled it by adding, "But you *are* secretive."

I wanted to deny it, but then I'd have had to tell him STUFF—and who knows what would happen to either of us if I did that? Ms. Sparks would probably have to turn us into toads.

We walked the rest of the way home in silence.

I'm not sure if he's talking to me anymore.

5:55 p.m.

Ash just brought over some leftover cake. Nobody has
leftover cake (especially not when it's a super-sticky,
scrumptious spicy orange cake made by his mom),
so I think it's a peace offering. As a counter peace
offering, I asked him to stay and watch a Harry Potter
movie with me.

8:32 p.m.

He just left, and we're still friends. There was a
slightly awkward moment when he asked me if I
was taking notes during one of the scenes. I told him
not to be RIDICULOUS. (Of course I was.)

Professor Snape might be a
make-believe wizard, but
he does seem to know
an awful lot about
potions. - - - ▷

84

9:11 p.m.

I must ask Amara where she got that dress.

10:01 p.m.

I wonder if I could pull off silver flares?

SUNDAY SEPTEMBER 26

4:23 p.m. Home

Spent the whole day in my bedroom with my
wand, trying to levitate things, TONS of things—
pajamas, hairbrush, my bear, this book, this pen,
etc. etc. No matter how hard I tried (very hard,
because once you start trying to make things fly,
it's very hard to stop), nothing went so much as a
micro-millimeter in the air. I thought my wand
might be broken or need rebooting or something.
I couldn't find any kind of ON/OFF switch, though,
so I gave it a really hard shake, but all that
happened was that I burned a hole in my pajama
bottoms. This magic stuff—*which I can't do*—is a
serious fire hazard.

4:43 p.m.

Dad just came up and asked for the millionth-zillionth time if I was okay and I said for the millionth-zillionth time that I was FINE. I was already feeling bad and then he started apologizing for the burn on my pajamas. "I must have lost concentration when I was ironing," he said. "I was probably thinking about your costume for the ball."

I wasn't really listening because I was too busy trying to figure out how to confess that I'd singed the pajamas, without mentioning wands or getting into trouble about using matches, and then he said, "How about a *witch* costume?"

I GASPED.

"Great idea, right?"

TERRIBLE IDEA.

"I could whip up a long, ragged cloak and buy some stick-on *warts* and we could draw some hairs on your chin—turn you into a real witchy witch."

RUDE.

"You'll need some striped tights ... like your school socks, but red!"

What?! So I can offend everyone in the school—*especially red-striped-sock-wearing ninth graders*—and the entire witching world? Has he no idea how SENSITIVE these people are?

"Oh." Dad stopped laughing and looked at me sadly. "You don't like that idea, do you?" *How could he tell??!* "Okay, okay, I'll think of something else.... I know, I'll make it a surprise."

I nodded weakly. I had NO WORDS.

Anything but a witch costume.

4:52 p.m.

Maybe not. Too scary.

TO-DO LIST

- REMIND DAD TO HURRY UP AND GET ME OUT OF THIS SCHOOL.
- Ask Blair how to do a loop-the-loop on a broom.
- Find three words that rhyme with armadillo—karmadillo? Llamadillo??
- Learn to cook.

- REMIND DAD AGAIN TO HURRY UP AND GET ME TRANSFERRED TO THE **ACADEMY** *BEFORE* HALLOWEEN.

5:01 p.m.

Okay. I'm going to go downstairs and be the PERFECT DAUGHTER and help with everything and CLEAN the kitchen, *then* I'm going to nag Dad about switching schools.

5:41 p.m.

What I would give for a cleaning-up spell right now. Speaking of spells, our English homework is to write a poem about the moon because Madam Binx says a) all poems are magical and there's nothing better for setting the scene for successful magic and b) everyone knows lunar spirits especially enjoy poetry.

8:33 p.m.

Still haven't ~~started~~ finished my homework. I'm not *sure* what kind of poem a lunar spirit would enjoy.

MONDAY SEPTEMBER 27

12:07 p.m. School

Bumped into Ms. Sparks after physics. She asked me how everything was going with a look of deep concern (possibly because my tie was on fire).

"Rr-r-really well," I stuttered, patting out the flames.

Ms. Sparks fixed me with a Piercing Look and asked me how it was *really* going. I confessed that levitation was not coming naturally and she told me not to be disheartened because the only way was UP. I felt a bit better. "And at least you don't have anything to worry about in math," she added. "No levitation going on in Mr. Smith's classroom."

I didn't feel better anymore.

1:10 p.m.

Blair's name was pulled out of Mrs. Slater's cauldron after lunch today and she's going to be the Queen of Mischief at the Halloween Ball! She's pretty smug about it. Puck says it's a BIG DEAL and it's been a witch tradition since the days of Minerva Moon (whoever she is). He's jealous because apparently the Queen* is not only allowed but is *expected* to prank-spell. *What*, I asked Puck, *is a PRANK-SPELL?* And he said it's exactly what it sounds like and looked at me like I was an especially dense **toadbrain**.

"You know, spells to make people at the party laugh. Silly stuff like, last Halloween, the King magicked all the seniors so they could only *hop* and their frogs so they could only *walk* and the year before that the Queen spell-swapped the teachers' clothes." Then he couldn't explain anymore because he was laughing so hard at the memory of Mr. Muddy wearing Ms. Sparks's dress, but I think I get it.

* Or KING obviously.

2:49 p.m.

In the end, the poem I read out loud in English was very short.

> **Light of the moon...**
> **Behind the cloud**
> **You seem very far away.**

    I pretended that it was so short because it was a haiku (?????), but it was really because I got so stressed reading the first verse aloud with everyone watching me that I had to ask Madam Binx if I could go to the bathroom instead of reading the rest.

8:15 p.m. Home

I have a *cunning plan* ... which is why I've spent the last hour sitting on the floor of my bedroom, working on my husky voice and coughing skills, instead of doing my homework and recording the phases of the moon. A week or two at home, hiding and stealth-practicing spelling and worrying about fractions, is the way to go.

In fact, it would probably be better for everyone if I became a HERMIT.

9:02 p.m.

Dad heard me "coughing"and came up to make me drink some medicine that was *almost* as disgusting as witch sausages because it would be "such a shame" if I were to miss school.

9:13 p.m.

I do actually feel quite sick now.

TUESDAY SEPTEMBER 28

6:03 p.m. Home

I forgot to take my diary with me to school today and I missed it *all day long*. I REFUSE to accept that Dad's got a point when he's says it's become my "security blanket." Ugh.

I talked to Stan A LOT, but he didn't talk back.

Winnie asked me if I was coming to lunch, but I said I had a packed lunch. She said I should still come and sit in the lunchroom with everyone else and that I couldn't "hide away somewhere scribbling in *that diary* forever." I one hundred percent was going to do that, but when I got to the line, Hunter and Blair and Izzi were in front of me, talking very loudly about how all the teachers were letting me get away with being

USELESS and why had I even been allowed to come to Extraordinary? So I decided that, after all, hiding in coat closets and ~~diarrizzing~~ scribbling is *wonderful.*

The thing is, Hunter and Blair and Izzi are right. I'm not like them, and even a **toadbrain** knows that at school, not being like everyone else is very much NOT a good thing. And it's worse at this school because I'm *never* going to be like everyone else because **I CAN'T DO MAGIC.** *Obviously.**

I miss my old school. I especially miss my old friends.

Dad's late coming home, and even if I can't talk to him about anything, I wish he'd hurry up and just *be* here.

6:50 p.m.

Dad just got home. He bought a spacehopper. WHY?

6:57 p.m.

Now he's bouncing around the yard. Who in their right mind *spacehops*????

* *Okay, I can manage to (mostly) stay on an ENCHANTED broom, but Blair's probably right when she says even a toadbrain could do that.*

7:07 p.m.

I take it all back: Spacehopping is my new favorite thing.

WEDNESDAY SEPTEMBER 29

11:10 a.m. School

It's been a VERY stressful morning. I was late because halfway to school I realized I'd forgotten my wand and I had to run home at broom-speed to get it. Found it! *Phew!* (Dad had put it in the silverware drawer beside the big spoons and the "other" chopsticks.) That meant I was late picking up Stan and he was the only class frog left in the frog cubbyholes in the main office. He looked very happy to be rescued from Mrs. Slater. I don't think she likes frogs much more than she likes children.

In the end, I was twenty minutes late, but Miss Lupo was in a good mood and just told me to sit down and stop sweating and that I'd have to catch up.

She was scrawling another one of her strange recipes
on the whiteboard.

Ingredients

- 1 sprig rosemary · · · ·
- 1 smashed clove poor man's treacle
- 1 tsp angelica
- 1 small bunch catnip
- 7 medium-sized cuckoo flower
  petals (fresh or dried)
- 1 vial tears of a baboon (if baboon tears
  are unavailable, substitute human tears)
- 1 tbsp runny honey
- 1 cookie (any variety) · · · ·

Take the poor man's treacle, angelica,
catnip, flower petals, and rosemary and crush
VIGOROUSLY in a pestle and mortar until the
consistency of toothpaste (this will take AT
LEAST ten minutes). Soak the paste in the
solution of tears and honey overnight or for longer.

"Okay! You'll find angelica, catnip, and rosemary in the school yards and all you have to do is prepare the potion on your own time and bring it into class on the first Tuesday after the full Frost Moon—always such a good day for concoctions! Simple! So easy that even you children can't mess it up!" I swear she was looking at me when she said that.

Puck, who'd somehow managed to turn his hair purple during the class, asked what the cookie was for, and Miss Lupo said it was just in case we got hungry after all the VIGOROUS CRUSHING and that, if anyone preferred cake, she was absolutely fine with that. Then she **WHOOSHED** us all out of the classroom because her ninth-grade class was waiting.

Wow, doesn't matter what school you go to, ninth graders are always scary.

I didn't get a chance to find out what the potion was *for....*

11:15 a.m.

I think I misjudged Blair!

She's just come to find me. At first, I thought it was so she could laugh at me for hiding in the first-floor cloak coat closet with Stan. To be fair, she did laugh at me, but then she showed me where the light switch was and explained she'd come to give me a copy of her notes from the potions class because I'd missed a lot of important stuff! She was only helping me "just this once," she said because she'd been in trouble with Lupo often enough to know it was no fun and they could all see I was *struggling* (which was hard to deny from the back of the coat closet, especially as Stan was nodding so hard, I thought his little froggy head was going to fall off).

I said thank you tons of times, and I was about to screw up my courage and ask her to show me how to loop-the-loop before the next **GO** match, when she announced she had better things to do than hang around with New Girls in coat closets and disappeared.

Anyway, once I'd gotten over how neat her handwriting was, I could see I really had missed *a lot.*

The second page was just the stuff I'd copied down off the board, but the whole first page was new to me.

Oh, and apparently it's a potion to get rid of SPOTS—finally something useful!

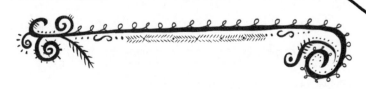

POTIONS NOTES

The most potent ingredient in this potion is the fingerlength of skeledrake root, which will be added, under supervision, to the other prepared ingredients in class. Bulbs grow five inches deep under the knotted roots of the great elm in Nightshade Glade and MUST be extracted following these instructions:

* Leave your house no earlier than eleven o'clock, nor later than quarter past on the night of the full Frost Moon.

* Take with you a small iron digging implement and a creature, strong in fang, to help you drag the root from the ground.

* POLITELY direct your broomstick to take you to Nightshade Glade, taking the as-the-crow-flies route.

* When you reach Nightshade Glade, first honor the spirit of the Frost Moon by singing an original song and then the spirits of the forest by performing an original dance.

* On the stroke of midnight, dig for the roots, and when you have found them, call upon your creature to drag them from their hiding place.

11:35 a.m.

I've read the instructions three times now and it's all very INTENSE. I'd just been planning on ducking into the **Sensible Store** and adding some poor man's treacle and cuckoo flowers to the weekly shopping list. Actually, that's a lie. I have no idea what I was planning, but definitely not *this*. And Nightshade Glade is much deeper into the forest than I've ever gone. I'm not sure I'd be brave enough to go that far in the middle of the day, much less at MIDNIGHT, but if everyone else is there getting their roots, too ... *maybe* it'll be fun?

Oh, well, it's not due for a while. I'm going to forget all about it for now.

11:43 a.m.

An *original song*.... Does that mean I have to *make one up*?

Dum-dee-dum-dee. Will there have to be words, too? I can't imagine the Frost Moon enjoying this very much.

11:54 a.m.

I wonder what kind of dance it has to be? I'm not really a dancing-in-moonlit-glades kind of girl.

Best to FORGET ABOUT IT for now.

12:15 p.m.

Where am I going to get a *"creature strong in fang"*? Would a puppy count?

TO-DO LIST: V. URGENT

- Ask Dad for the millionth-zillionth time if I can PLEASE have a puppy.
- Remind Dad for the millionth-zillionth time to get me transferred to the **Academy** ASAP.

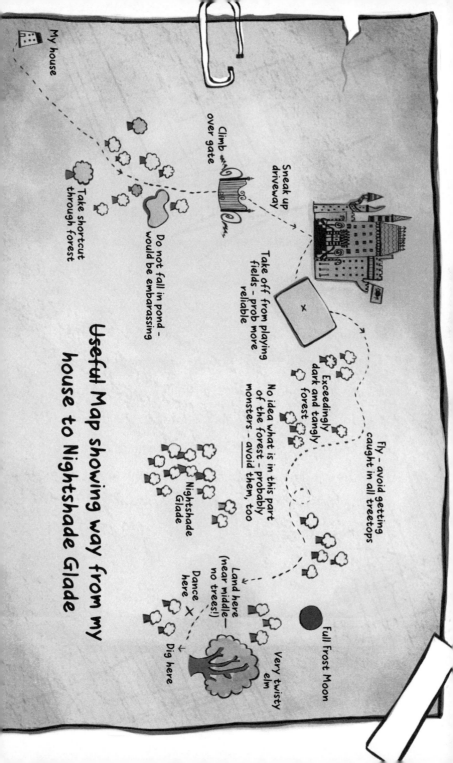

THURSDAY SEPTEMBER 30

10:52 a.m. School

Professor Agu brought a miniature pig named Excalibur into zoology!

Unfortunately, there's now a miniature pig on the loose on the school grounds. It really wasn't my fault. I was only joking when I said I wanted to see pigs fly. I didn't know Puck would take me seriously and I didn't know the window was open. Blair says she hopes it turns up before it meets Professor Crisp's python. I *think* she's joking.

2:43 p.m.

First history class with Professor Crisp who is even older than Mrs. Slater. In fact, he is so EXTREMELY old, I suspect he's lived through most of what he's teaching us. He didn't seem to have a python with him.... I hope it hasn't gone on a pig hunt.

I can't concentrate—I'm worrying about Excalibur.

History homework:

> *Write a 300-word essay on witchcraft during the Roman period, with particular reference to witch gladiators. Extra credit will be given for illustrations.*

11:59 p.m. Home

Too worried about Excalibur to sleep.

FRIDAY OCTOBER 1

9:03 a.m. School

Met the seventh-grade class frog on the way to registration and I have FROG ENVY. It's a neon-green tree frog named Pablo and he's the cutest, most upbeat ~~amfibbeean~~ hoppy-thing I've ever seen.

I feel *so bad* for Stan.

10:56 a.m.

Just got out of PE, and even though I had to give Fabi back his lucky sock after he fell off his broom three times in five minutes, I *still* scored FIVE goals!!!!!

Even Blair, captain of the Dragons, congratulated me. "Great job, Bea! What a FLUKE! So sorry about the injury." Now that I know her better, I'm sure she hadn't meant to crash me into the turret—it was a rough game.

Final score:

DODOS: 43	DRAGONS: 42

One hundred percent worth the concussion.

6:13 p.m. Home

I've got a bump the size of an EGG on my head. Dad has a bump on his head, too, because he got caught in a mini-storm of hailstones the size of ONIONS as he was spacehopping home after a happy day studying lightning scorch marks on the UnCommon, so we're both sitting here with packets of frozen peas on our heads and I'm trying to dodge his questions about my homework.

"Just some chemistry," I say vaguely. My peas were getting warm with the effort not to tell him EVERYTHING. I'd tried to distract him by mentioning that I'd seen a triple rainbow over the school bell tower.

He got very excited—apparently, it's incredibly rare but not *impossible* (unlike some of the things I've seen at Extraordinary). Then I told him I really NEEDED a puppy ASAP, one with teeth, and he blinked and looked a little sad and said *he* was always here for me to talk to if I was lonely.

8:52 p.m.

"Still awake, Bea?" Dad pops his head around my bedroom door. "There's something I need to tell you."

"What?" I ask suspiciously because he's got his sheepish face on.

"It's um … good news … and um … bad news."

"Can you start with the good news?" I say, because even though my head's gone back to its normal shape, it's been a very tough day, and maybe he's reconsidered about the puppy.

"I sent off the application for you to change schools—"

"DAD! THANK YOU!" I yell and jump out of bed to give him a hug.

No more rhyming spells, no more levitation, no more YUCKY witch sausages, no more hiding in the broom cupboard!

I am so happy.

9:33 p.m.

I am NOT happy anymore.

The bad news was VERY BAD indeed.

It's true that Dad sent off the change-schools-application, but instead of sending it to the **Academy**, he sent it to a very important cloud expert in ~~Casz~~ Kazakhstan!

"I'm so sorry," he said, sitting on my bed, pulling a squashed packet of cookies out of his pocket and offering me one. "I only found out just now when Professor Iskakov called me. It was just a tiny mix-up—I was distracted by the hailstones—it could have happened to anyone."

Oh, Dad!

"I'll send a new application tomorrow," he said. "I really am sorry."

"Sorry enough to buy me a puppy?"

"Not quite." He handed me another cookie instead. "Come on, Bea," he said in his most persuasive-parent voice. "Extraordinary can't be that bad. Why don't you write a list of all the things you like and make the best of it for a little longer?"

That is really ANNOYING advice.

11:32 p.m.

Couldn't get to sleep because I've been thinking about "how to make the best of it," so I've stayed up making a tiny yellow Dodo bib for Stan to wear at the next

GO match out of an old pair of underwear. Pretty sure seventh grade Pablo doesn't have one of those.

Stan is going to the top of my list....

~~LIST OF THINGS TO DO WHILE I AM STUCK AT EXTRAORDINARY~~ MAKING THE BEST OF IT LIST

- Hang out with Stan (hopefully not always in a broom cupboard).
- Play as many **GO** matches as possible.
- Learn to make my own packed lunches so I never have to eat witch food again. Ever.
- Teach Winnie and Amara and Fabi and Puck how to ride a bike.
- Make up a very good original song and dance routine to entertain the lunar spirits on the night of the Frost Moon.
- Try to levitate something/anything just one time before I leave!

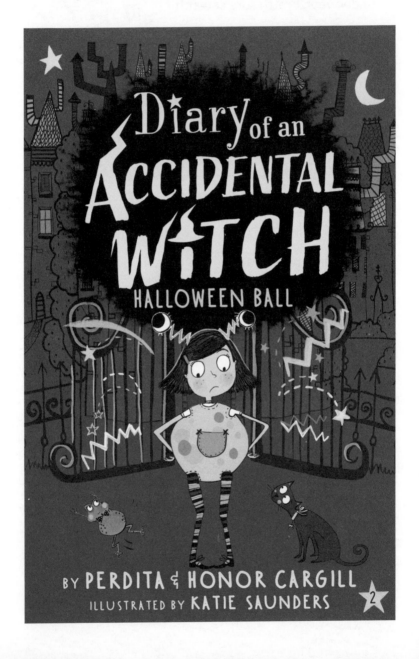

11:02 a.m. School

Dad finally sent the application for me to move to the **Academy**, where there are no witches AT ALL. But for now, I'm stuck at Extraordinary, it's only break time, and I've already had to retreat to my favorite broom cupboard with Stan the class frog for a little rest.

I don't think anyone—except maybe Winnie—likes starting Monday with double physics (aka wand work), but it's extra hard if you can't make anything go up in the air. And now I'm panicking about potions. Even if the **Academy** replies at broomstick speed, it's probably not going to be fast enough to get me out of doing my Frost Moon homework!

1:55 p.m.

Have just spent forever searching for Professor Agu's miniature pig, Excalibur, but nobody has seen him since he went flying out the classroom window last Thursday.

Fabi says he's probably having a wonderful time in the Deep, Dark Forest, but now I'm very worried about WEREWOLVES and it's all my fault! Pretty sure I wouldn't have to worry about this kind of thing at the **Academy**.

The Extraordinary: Halloween Issue 1

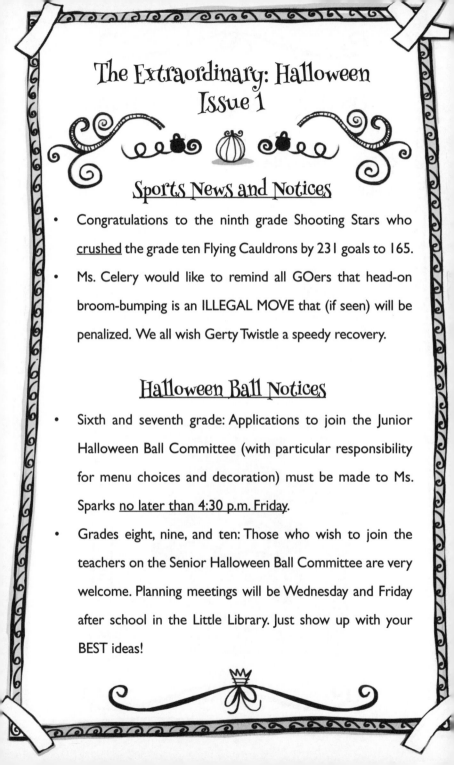

Sports News and Notices

- Congratulations to the ninth grade Shooting Stars who <u>crushed</u> the grade ten Flying Cauldrons by 231 goals to 165.

- Ms. Celery would like to remind all GOers that head-on broom-bumping is an ILLEGAL MOVE that (if seen) will be penalized. We all wish Gerty Twistle a speedy recovery.

Halloween Ball Notices

- Sixth and seventh grade: Applications to join the Junior Halloween Ball Committee (with particular responsibility for menu choices and decoration) must be made to Ms. Sparks <u>no later than 4:30 p.m. Friday</u>.

- Grades eight, nine, and ten: Those who wish to join the teachers on the Senior Halloween Ball Committee are very welcome. Planning meetings will be Wednesday and Friday after school in the Little Library. Just show up with your BEST ideas!

Quick-fire Q & A with Ms. Sparks!

Q: Favorite time of the year?

A: Halloween of course!

Q: Favorite pet?

A: *Long pause while principcal thinks* ~~Um, I had a dog when I was little, a cockerpoo named Bubble~~ ZEPHYR OF COURSE!

Q: Favorite joke?

A: What goes cackle, cackle, bonk? A witch laughing her head off!

Thank you, Ms. Sparks!

Dear Agony Witch

Dear Agony Witch,

X in my class is a twin. Y in my class is also a twin. X and Y keep swapping places and then laughing at me when I call them by the wrong name. While the rest of the class finds this very funny, I feel it is undermining my authority. I cannot tell which witch is which. What should I do?

Yours,

A Worried Teacher

Dear Worried Teacher,

I suggest you turn one into a warthog, easily distinguished from a witch. Problem solved. Have a great year.

Love,

Agony Witch x

TUESDAY OCTOBER 5

3:25 p.m. School

"I hope you're all doing well with the preparations for that potion I gave you last week," says Miss Lupo, demonstrating the best way to use a pestle and mortar. "Get busy collecting your tears of a baboon, cuckoo flowers, and poor man's treacle, and don't forget that the night of the full Frost Moon is an excellent one for magical concoctions."

And the best night of the year to dig for skeledrake roots!

I catch Blair's eye and smile shyly. She might not have been the most welcoming witch in the class when I came to Extraordinary, and she doesn't give off a very friendly vibe, but if she hadn't given me those extra notes when I missed class, I'd never had known that I had to go to Nightshade Glade at midnight and dig for skeledrakes while performing a SONG AND DANCE routine for the lunar spirits!

3:29 p.m.

Worrying a little because I'm even worse at singing and dancing than I am at potions. Must figure out how to get to Nightshade Glade.

ABOUT THE AUTHOR*

Bea Black is eleven years old and has recently
moved to Little Spellshire, where she lives with
her dad, a weather scientist. She has no pets,
but has been on class frog rotation this semester.
Her lifelong dream is to get a puppy.
This is Bea's first diary.

*With a little help from Perdita and Honor Cargill!